Get lost
in
a good
book!

Patricia Polacco

For the Love of Autumn

For the

Love of Autumn

Patricia
Polacco

Philomel
Books

When Danielle saw Autumn for the very first time, she held that tiny kitten in the palm of her hand. She marveled at how perfect and small that creature was. Danielle named her Autumn because it was almost Halloween. It was love at first sight.

"Poor little thing, you look like you haven't eaten for quite a while," Danielle said as she gave her warm milk and a bit of food. Then Danielle made a special little bed for her to sleep in. She set out water and kibble and a litter box. Danielle looked forward to coming home so that she could hold and pet Autumn. As each day passed, she loved that little kitten more and more!

Soon Autumn was scurrying around the apartment. She tipped over the trash, pulled the laundry out of the hamper, knocked all of the pencils and papers off the desk and jumped out at Danielle's ankles as she walked by.

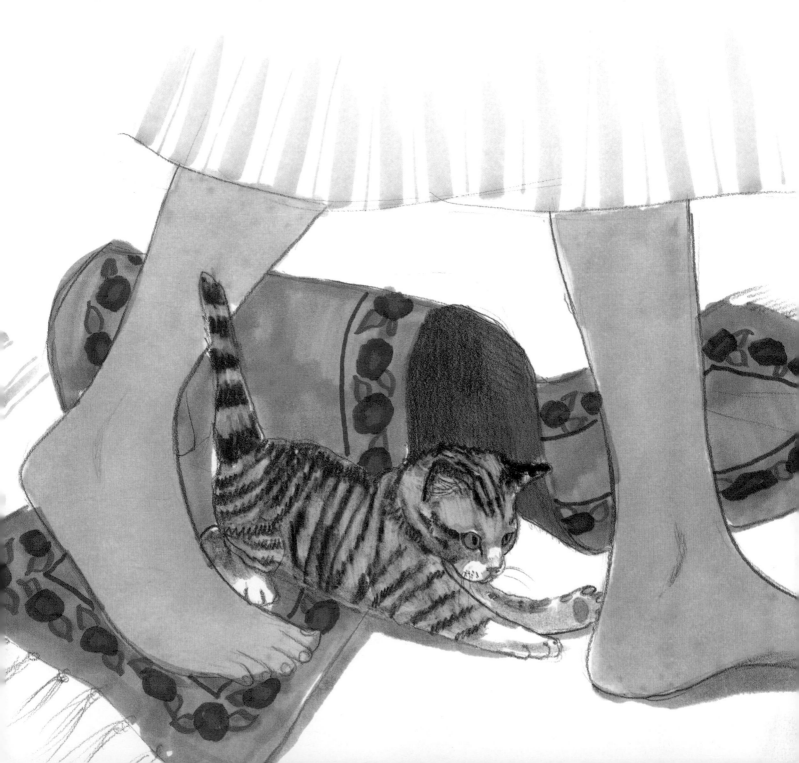

Danielle was a student teacher. When she came home from school and tried to correct her students' papers, Autumn would lie right in the middle of them. After dinner Danielle would pop corn and they'd sit on the sofa together and watch TV, and at bedtime Autumn would curl up in Danielle's arms and purr and purr and purr until they both drifted off to sleep.

One day, as Danielle opened her mail, she squealed with delight. "Oh, Autumn, I got a teaching job! It's in Port Townsend, Washington. I've always wanted to live by the sea, and Port Townsend is right by the sea."

When Danielle packed for the move, Autumn hid in the packing boxes. She wrestled with the packing shreds and pounced on the Bubble Wrap, popping it as she landed on it.

Danielle and Autumn drove together all the way up the coast of California, through Oregon and into the state of Washington. Finally, as they came over the crest of a tall hill, there it was . . . the beautiful little village right next to the sea.

The school had arranged for Danielle to rent a lovely cottage right on the bay. An enchanted cottage, she thought when she saw it.

Autumn loved her new little house. The very first thing she did was disappear right up the chimney. When the kitten finally came down, she was covered with soot and ashes.

Autumn helped Danielle unpack! She got inside every paper bag that hit the floor, jumped into every box that was emptied and almost knocked over a stack of Danielle's favorite china.

That first evening, Autumn and Danielle sat on her sofa eating popcorn and looking out the window at the sea as a warm fire crackled in the fireplace.

Danielle loved her new school and adored each and every one of her students.

"Miss Parks," they asked her one day, "are you married?"

"No, not yet … but someday, when just the right man comes along, I will be."

"How will you know he's the one?" one of the children asked.

"I'll hear the sound of thunder, smell jasmine, and the wind will blow his hair. I'll know that he is exactly the one!"

"Oh, Miss Parks, do you think he's out there somewhere?" little Mary Proctor asked.

"Indeed I do. I can just feel it," Miss Parks answered wistfully.

Yes, Danielle Parks loved her students and she loved her little cottage almost as much. She planted a cottage garden. She pulled weeds and fertilized the lawn and trimmed the hedges. She even painted the wonderful old trellis.

As for Autumn . . . she loved the place. She raced about the garden, stalked butterflies in the flower beds, climbed the apple trees and even perched herself atop the trellis so she could watch the birds in the new birdbath.

Both of them settled into their new life in that little cottage by the sea.

One afternoon, when Danielle got home from school, a terrible storm was raging. There was thunder, the sky was black and the raindrops, big as bumblebees, hit the roof with a pinging sound. Autumn didn't greet Danielle at the door like she always did.

Danielle searched the house but couldn't find Autumn anywhere! She called her next-door neighbors to see if they had seen her.

"Oh, she's probably hiding out somewhere with this fierce storm," her neighbor reassured her. But Danielle was worried.

Late that night, Danielle heard a scratching sound at the door. She opened it and there was Autumn! She was soaking wet, and her tail had a huge gash in it that was bleeding. Danielle reached for her, but Autumn shrank from her touch and ran into the night.

Danielle ran after her. She walked around the neighborhood in driving rain, calling, "Autumn! Autumn!"

But Autumn didn't come. She had completely disappeared.

When Danielle left for school that morning, she left the back door ajar in the hope that Autumn would come home.

All that day at school, her students noticed that something was wrong.

"Miss Parks, where do you think Autumn could be?" Jamie Ross asked after Danielle told the class why she was so worried.

"I think all of us should come to Miss Parks' after school today and look for Autumn," Jerome Bolton announced.

Kaleb Dirks stepped up. "Yeah, some of us can take the beach. You guys can look up in the woods on the hill, and you girls stop at every house to see if anyone has seen her!"

The children were true to their word. They all came to Miss Parks' cottage. They launched a search that would shame the FBI, but alas, there was no Autumn to be found.

Days stretched into weeks.

Danielle cried almost every night just thinking of Autumn. There had been rumors that a mountain lion had been seen, and her cottage was very near a state park where one had been sighted. Danielle feared the very worst!

She walked around the little cottage and cried whenever she looked at anything that was Autumn's. She picked up Autumn's empty little bed and ran her hands over it. She looked at Autumn's paw prints still on the windowsill. She didn't eat popcorn anymore, nor sit and watch the sea by the fire. Danielle's heart was broken.

Finally Danielle put away Autumn's food and water bowls. She took all of her toys and put them in a bin in the laundry room, but she couldn't bear to put Autumn's bed away. She couldn't bear to brush Autumn's fur off her sofa cushions. Danielle ached from the loss of the heartbeat of her little cottage, because to her, that is what Autumn was.

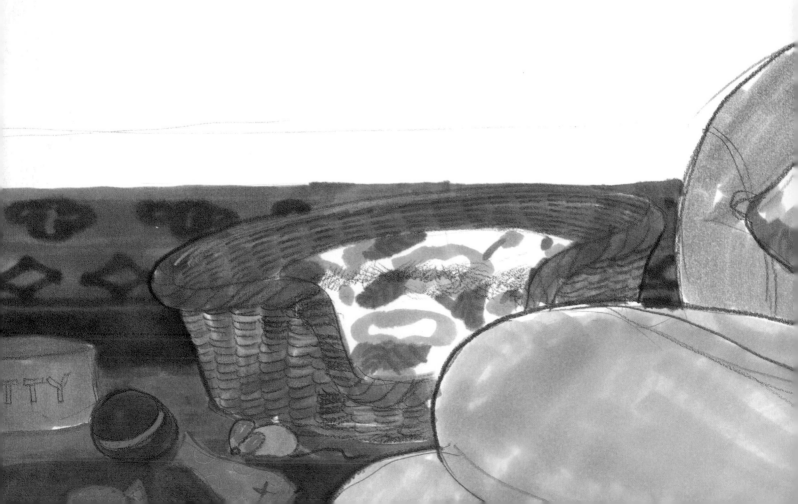

On Saturday, Danielle and her students planted a small bed of flowers where Autumn used to lie in the shade of the apple tree. The children had polished rocks and placed them in a circle on the ground.

"We'll always call this Autumn's garden," Benny Barber whispered softly.

"I think she would have loved that," Miss Parks said wistfully.

Just as the children were about to leave, there was a small sound and something jumped off the trellis into Miss Parks' arms.

It was Autumn!

"Autumn," Danielle cried out as she hugged her. "Where have you been?"

The children surrounded them and gave them a group hug.

"You have been gone for six whole weeks!"

"But Miss Parks, she doesn't look like she's been in the woods. Look! Her fur is shiny and clean. She looks nice and healthy!" Benny Barber noticed.

"And her tail," Danielle said as she examined it. "There was a horrible gash on it the night she ran off. It looks like it has been shaved . . . and some stitches taken in it. Someone has taken wonderful care of Autumn!"

Autumn stuck close to home for the next week, until one day she left again, only to return the following weekend wearing a flea collar.

"Well, for goodness' sake, who put this flea collar on you?" Danielle wondered as she took it off. "I have a collar for you, sweetie. Pink . . . your favorite color."

Then one day, Autumn went away again and came back two days later with a phone number scrawled on the collar.

"Children," Danielle announced in class that morning. "Someone has put their phone number on MY CAT'S COLLAR!"

"Wow!" they all exclaimed.

"We have a real mystery on our hands," Johnnie Carter said. He thought for a minute. "Someone must think that Autumn is their cat."

"Well, she's MY cat!" Danielle asserted.

"Miss Parks, you have to call that number. You have to tell the person she is your cat!" Benny Barber insisted.

That evening, Danielle paced the floor. She wasn't accustomed to calling someone whom she had never seen before. But Autumn circled the phone and kept looking up at her as if she wanted her to call.

"Well, here goes," Danielle said as she dialed the number.

A voice answered the phone.

"Yes," Danielle started. "Uh . . . well . . . my cat seems to have your phone number on her collar."

"Oh, thank God. You found Stormy!" The voice sounded relieved. "I've been so worried."

"Stormy? Her name isn't Stormy. Her name is Autumn!" Danielle felt her face flush.

"Oh, no. I named her Stormy because she came to my house on a terrible stormy night, badly injured. Her tail had been slashed. Probably a mountain lion."

"No . . . sir . . . you don't understand. I have had Autumn since she was a kitten. She disappeared on a stormy night from my home. She's MY cat!"

"Well, if she's so precious to you, then why was she out in such a terrible storm?"

Danielle quickly hung up. "What nerve!" she snorted. "What a rude man!"

When she told her class about the phone call, they were all intrigued. They spent a whole afternoon doing drawings of what they imagined the rude man looked like.

That afternoon, Autumn came in the house with a note attached to her collar. When Danielle opened it, it simply read, "Please accept my apologies. I didn't mean to be rude."

Danielle quickly sat down and wrote a note back.

"I apologize as well. Perhaps I was rude too." She attached the note to Autumn's collar and sent her out the door.

Two afternoons later, Autumn came back with another note attached.

"Since we both care so deeply for this little kitty, perhaps we can share her. I live alone and truly love her company."

When Danielle shared the most recent note with her class, all of them decided that she needed to invite the note writer over to her house so she could meet him.

"Oh, children, I'm not in the habit of inviting a perfect stranger to my home."

"But Miss Parks, he's obviously a lonely old man and he can't be a bad person if he helped Autumn, could he?" Benny Barber said.

"All right then. I'm going to ask him to stop by this Saturday," she said.

"Oh, can we come too?" her entire class pleaded. "We want to meet him!"

Miss Parks agreed, and all that afternoon the children helped her compose the invitation.

Saturday was a dark and rainy day, but every kid in Danielle's class was at her house by early afternoon. All of them had their faces pasted to the front window to see what he would be like when he came to the door.

Every time a car drove up, the children
would shriek with delight, only to sigh when
the car passed by.

Finally, just when it looked like he wasn't
really coming and they had turned away, there
was a knock at the door.

Autumn ran to the door. As Miss Parks opened it, there was a clap of thunder. The wind came up and blew the trellis so that the jasmine vine unraveled and a clump of it fell into his hands. Then another gust blew his hair into his eyes.

"Miss Parks, I'm Stephen Norton. I think we share a wonderful little cat."

Autumn sprang into his arms and purred and purred and purred. Danielle beamed as she gazed into his face.

"This little cat is the heartbeat of my house," Mr. Norton said softly as he caressed Autumn.

A clap of thunder echoed over the bay and the wind caught the jasmine vine and scattered blossoms everywhere.

Why, her students whispered to one another, "Miss Parks has found the very one."

And Autumn had found them both.

Stephen Norton and Danielle Parks were married that next spring. They shared not only the enchanted cottage by the sea, but walks on the beach, evenings by the fire eating popcorn, and most of all, their love of Autumn.

In loving memory of my dearest Missy.
She was the heart of my household,
my friend and mirthful companion
of twenty years.

Patricia Lee Gauch, Editor

PHILOMEL BOOKS
A division of Penguin Young Readers Group.
Published by The Penguin Group.
Penguin Group (USA) Inc., 375 Hudson Street, New York, NY 10014, U.S.A.
Penguin Group (Canada), 90 Eglinton Avenue East, Suite 700, Toronto, Ontario M4P 2Y3, Canada
(a division of Pearson Penguin Canada Inc.).
Penguin Books Ltd, 80 Strand, London WC2R 0RL, England.
Penguin Ireland, 25 St. Stephen's Green, Dublin 2, Ireland (a division of Penguin Books Ltd.).
Penguin Group (Australia), 250 Camberwell Road, Camberwell, Victoria 3124, Australia (a division of Pearson Australia Group Pty Ltd).
Penguin Books India Pvt Ltd, 11 Community Centre, Panchsheel Park, New Delhi - 110 017, India.
Penguin Group (NZ), 67 Apollo Drive, Rosedale, North Shore 0632, New Zealand (a division of Pearson New Zealand Ltd).
Penguin Books (South Africa) (Pty) Ltd, 24 Sturdee Avenue, Rosebank, Johannesburg 2196, South Africa.
Penguin Books Ltd, Registered Offices: 80 Strand, London WC2R 0RL, England.

Published simultaneously in Canada.   Manufactured in China by South China Printing Co. Ltd.
Design by Semadar Megged.   Text set in 16-point Adobe Jenson.   The illustrations are rendered in pencils and markers.

Library of Congress Cataloging-in-Publication Data is available upon request.

ISBN 978-0-399-24541-1
1 3 5 7 9 10 8 6 4 2